All About Me

It's My Birthday!

By Meg Gaertner

level 1 little blue readers

www.littlebluehousebooks.com

Little Blue House is distributed by North Star Editions:
sales@northstareditions.com | 888-417-0195

Produced for Little Blue House by Red Line Editorial.

Photographs ©: kali9/iStockphoto, cover, 12–13; Wavebreakmedia/iStockphoto, 4, 10–11; ArtMarie/iStockphoto, 7; Rawpixel/iStockphoto, 9; junce/iStockphoto, 15; kongkanglp/Shutterstock Images, 16 (top left); monkeybusinessimages/iStockphoto, 16 (top right); mvp64/iStockphoto, 16 (bottom left); Lopolo/Shutterstock Images, 16 (bottom right)

Library of Congress Control Number: 2019943159

ISBN
978-1-64619-001-0 (hardcover)
978-1-64619-040-9 (paperback)
978-1-64619-079-9 (ebook pdf)
978-1-64619-118-5 (hosted ebook)

Printed in the United States of America
Mankato, MN
012020

About the Author

Meg Gaertner enjoys reading, writing, dancing, and being outside. She lives in Minnesota.

Table of Contents

It's My Birthday!

It is my birthday.

I have a party.

It is my birthday.

I have balloons.

balloon

It is my birthday.

I have friends over.

It is my birthday.

I have family over.

It is my birthday.

I have candles.

candles

It is my birthday.

I have cake.

cake

Glossary

balloons

family

cake

party

Index